This book belongs to

....

....

To Mark, James,
Joseph and Jessica.
 J.H.

For Poppy and Lewis
and, as ever, my lovely
wife Tiziana.
  J.B-B.

This edition first published in 2007 by Alligator Books Ltd.

cupcake

Cupcake is an imprint of Alligator Books Ltd.
Gadd House, Arcadia Avenue, London N3 2JU

Text © Julia Hubery 2003
Illustrations © John Bendall-Brunello 2003

1 3 5 7 9 10 8 6 4 2

The right of Julia Hubery and John Bendall-Brunello to be identified
as the author and illustrator of this work has been asserted by them
in accordance with the Copyright, Designs and Patents Act, 1988.
A CIP record for this title is available from the British Library.

ISBN: 978-1-84750-185-1

Printed in Malaysia

The Naughtiest Piglet

Julia Hubery

John Bendall-Brunello

cupcake

It had been a hot day on the farm, and Mother Pig
was counting her piglets, ready for bed.
"One, two, three . . . stand still! . . . four, five, six . . .
don't wriggle! . . . seven, eight . . . where's Naughty?
Does anyone know where Naughty is?"
Eight little piglets shook their heads.
Mother Pig sighed. "I suppose I'll have
to go and find him – yet again!"

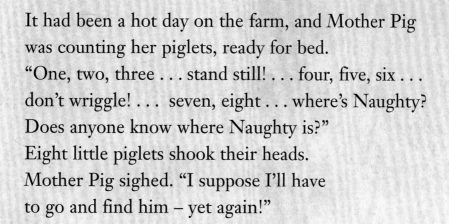
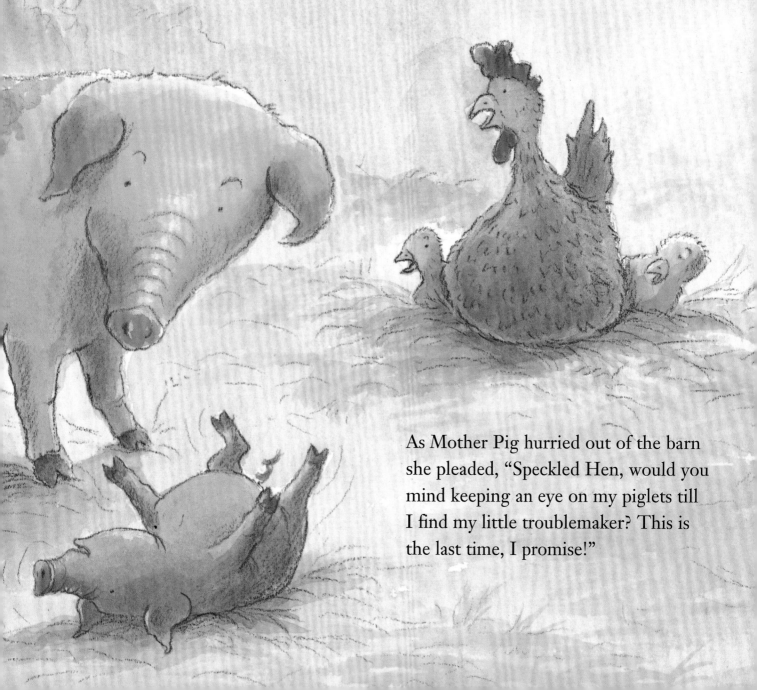

As Mother Pig hurried out of the barn
she pleaded, "Speckled Hen, would you
mind keeping an eye on my piglets till
I find my little troublemaker? This is
the last time, I promise!"

Mother Pig went to ask Brown Cow, who stood
chewing a mouthful of grass by the farm gate.
"Good evening, Brown Cow," greeted
Mother Pig. "Have you seen my
naughtiest piglet anywhere?"

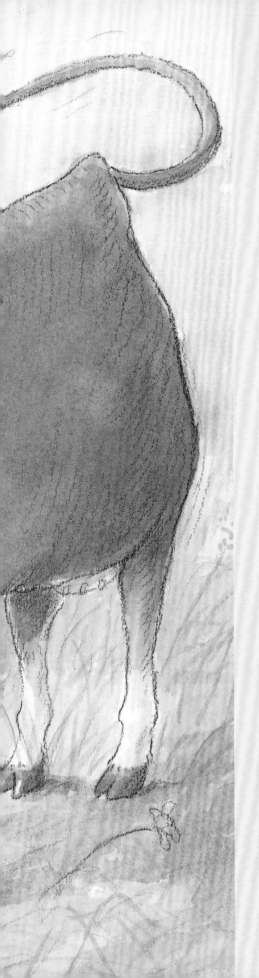

"I'm afraid I have," nodded
Brown Cow. "Your Naughty
wanted to help the milkmaid . . .

. . . the next I saw of him, he came dashing out of the parlour in a milky mess!"

"And where is he now?" asked Mother Pig.
"He headed for Major's field, and I think you'd
better find him quickly!" advised Brown Cow.
"When I do find him, I hope to see a very sorry
little piglet!" said Mother Pig, rushing off.

"Good evening, Major,"
said Mother Pig.
"Have you seen my
naughtiest piglet lately?"

"Madam," said Major, "I've seen the naughtiest, the cheekiest, and the RUDEST piglet ever . . .

. . . he *barged* into my field,

dived into my water trough,

then *rolled* in my best clover. No manners at all!"

"I'm so sorry, Major," said Mother Pig,
"and I hope my Naughty will be
even sorrier when I find him."
"IF you find him, Madam! The silly thing
ran off towards the duckpond."

"The duckpond!" cried Mother Pig. "But
he can't swim! Oh that worrisome piglet!"

"Good evening, White Ducks," said Mother Pig, skidding to a muddy stop at the pond edge. "It looks like my naughtiest piglet has been here. Can you tell me where he went?"

"It's actually NOT a very good evening," snapped the eldest duck. "It's a very HOT evening, and it's also a very DRY evening. Your naughtiest piglet has indeed been here . . .

. . . but since he churned our lovely clear pond into a murky mess, he's the SLIMIEST piglet!

I don't know where
he went next, and
I don't care either,"
said the eldest duck.

"When I find that piglet I expect him to be
VERY VERY sorry!" muttered Mother Pig,
as she followed the muddy trotter prints up
the hill towards Gruff Billy's field.

"Good evening, Gruff Billy," panted Mother Pig.
"Well, good evening, Mother Pig," said Gruff Billy. "You're
going to ask me if I've seen your naughtiest piglet, aren't you?"
"And have you?" asked Mother Pig.
"I certainly have seen your piglet. I have seen TOO MUCH
of your piglet. I've seen your piglet everywhere . . .

. . . everywhere he shouldn't be!
I've seen him in the kennel . . .

. . . in the sheep-pen . . .

. . . in the hen-house . . .

. . . even in the farmhouse . . .

. . . and worst of all . . .

...in MY field!

And I don't want to see him again for
a LONG time," announced Gruff Billy.
"Where, oh where can he be?" squealed Mother
Pig as she toiled wearily back towards the old barn.
"I better check the haystack. That's where
I used to hide when I was a piglet in trouble,"
she sighed. "He may be a pest, but he's
my pest. I do hope he's there."

The naughtiest piglet was hiding in a dark corner of the barn, sobbing into the hay.

"I wish I wasn't so much trouble!" he whimpered. "I'll never be able to go home. I'll have to hide here for *ever*!"

Suddenly he heard his mother coming, and he burrowed deeper into the hay to hide.

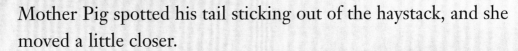

Mother Pig spotted his tail sticking out of the haystack, and she
moved a little closer.

"I wish my naughtiest piglet wasn't *so* naughty," she said. "I wish
he'd be more thoughtful, and I wish he'd learn some manners,"
she sighed. "But most of all, I wish he'd come back to me."

There was a muffled squeal from the haystack.
"I'm sorry, Mum," said a small voice.
Then the naughtiest piglet wriggled and wiggled
until he was snout to snout with Mother Pig . . .

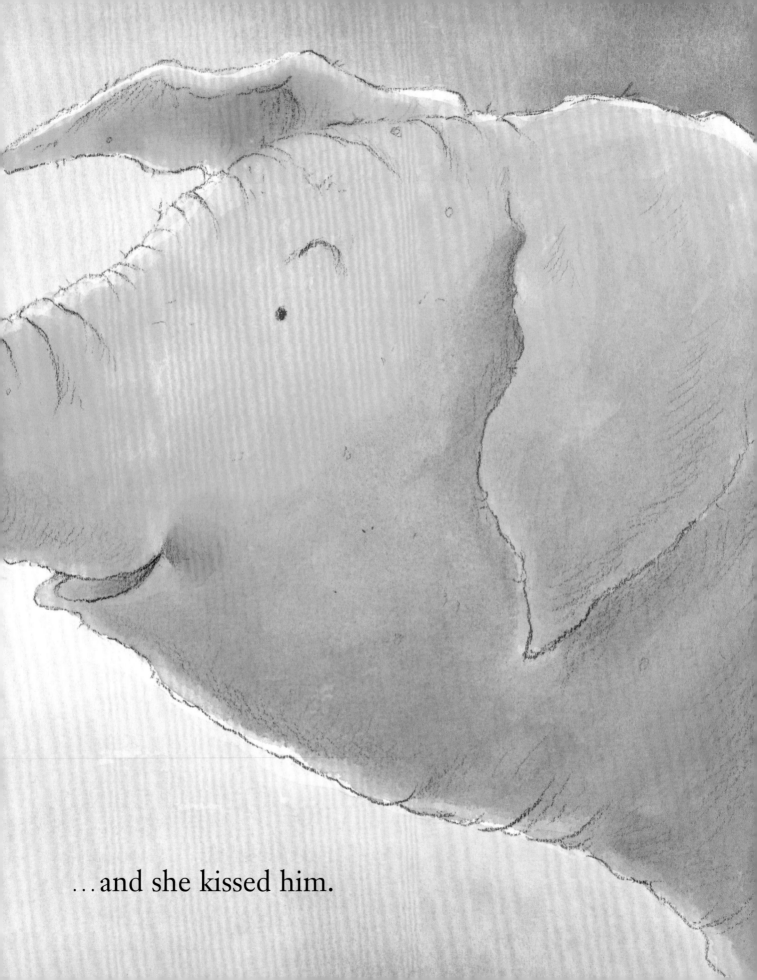

…and she kissed him.